To: Eric

Happy Birthday

From: Tom Wagner

CLAIRE SCHUMACHER

BRAVE LILY

WILLIAM MORROW AND COMPANY, INC., NEW YORK

For Pamela Pollack, my editor

Library of Congress Cataloging in Publication Data
Schumacher, Claire. Brave Lily. Summary: Young frog Lily sets out bravely to rescue
her brother Freddy, whose expectations of being kissed by a girl and turned into a prince
have had a surprising result. 1. Children's stories, American. [1. Frogs—Fiction. 2.
Courage—Fiction. 3. Brothers and sisters—Fiction] I. Title.
PZ7.S3914Br 1985 [E] 84-29616
ISBN 0-688-04962-1 / ISBN 0-688-04963-X (lib. bdg.)

In the moonlight around the pond,
the frogs listen to stories.

Uncle Frog tells one about the Terrible Man who eats frog legs. "How awful," shudders Lily. "I do not like those kinds of stories."

Then Aunt Frog tells about the frog who is kissed by a beautiful girl and turns into a prince. "That's the life for me," thinks Lily's brother Freddy.

That night Freddy
dreams about his castle.
He smiles in his sleep.

Lily dreams that the Terrible Man is visiting their pond.
She wakes up crying.

"Don't be afraid," Mother Frog whispers. "It's easy to recognize
the Terrible Man. He always wears a beret. Now that you know this,
you will never let him catch you."

The next morning the other little frogs are swimming and diving, but Freddy doesn't join in. "I could be a prince," he moans, "if a beautiful girl would kiss me."

"Freddy," says Mother, "isn't it nice enough being a frog?"

"No," says Freddy. "I want to be a prince."

Freddy sees a girl walking down the road near the pond.
"Look, Lily. Here comes my princess."

Before Lily can stop him, Freddy lies down in the middle of the road. "Are you crazy?" asks Lily. "What are you doing?"

"I'm pretending to be sick," says Freddy, "so the beautiful girl will feel sorry for me and kiss me!"

"*Ick!* A dead frog." The girl jumps over Freddy and runs away. "Hey, princess," he calls after her, "how about a kiss?"

Somebody else is coming down the road. "I'll try again," Freddy says. "To become a prince you have to take chances." "No, Freddy, wait!" cries Lily. But it is too late. Freddy has already closed his eyes.

Hands lift him and a boy's voice says, "Poor frog. You must be hurt. I'll bring you home and take care of you."

"Oh, no, no," gasps Lily. "The Terrible Man has come. He is wearing a beret and Freddy doesn't see it."

As fast as she can, Lily jumps
and runs after the bicycle.

"We're home," says the boy.
"Now I can fix you up."

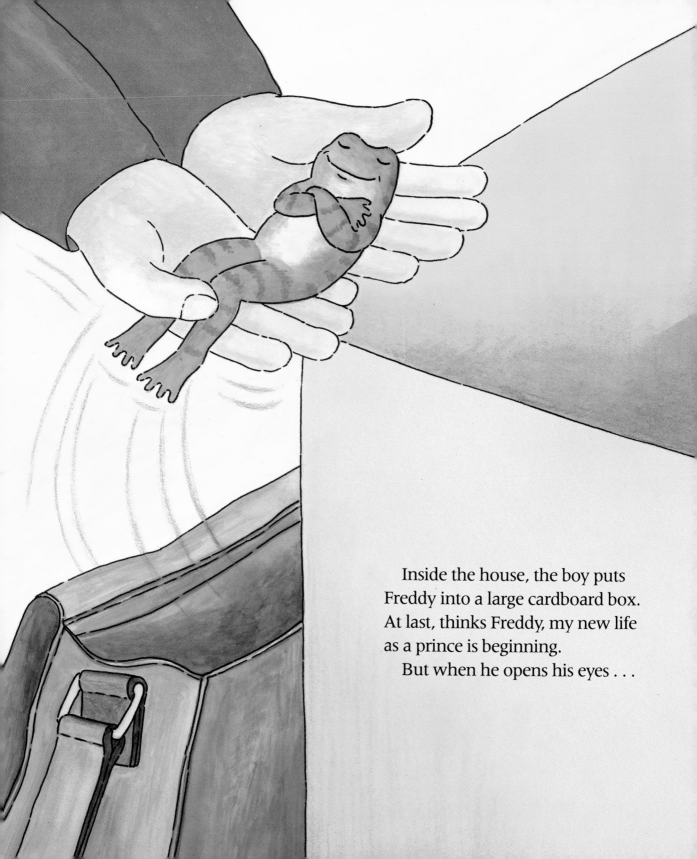

Inside the house, the boy puts
Freddy into a large cardboard box.
At last, thinks Freddy, my new life
as a prince is beginning.
But when he opens his eyes . . .

. . . he is alone. The floor of his castle feels very hard.
"I hope my princess hurries up," says Freddy.
"This isn't anything like the castle in Aunt Frog's story."

Outside the window Lily jumps and falls, and jumps and falls again.

But then she sees the vine growing right to the windowsill. Up and up she climbs . . .

. . . till she can peek in the window. "Oh, no," Lily cries. "The Terrible Man is getting ready to eat Freddy." The boy gives Freddy a plate of crumbs and apple peels and a pan of water.

Remembering the wonderful food in Aunt Frog's story, Freddy's mouth waters.

But when he tastes the dry crumbs—*ugh!*

"I don't like living in a castle," says Freddy.
"A prince's food isn't nearly as good as
Mother's flies. And there is no one to play
with. Poor me," wails Freddy. "I will never
see Mother and Lily again."

"Poor little frog," says the boy. "You didn't
touch your food. I'll try to find something
else for you in the kitchen."

Brave Lily. As soon as the boy leaves she slips inside the
window, slides down the curtains, crawls over the carpet . . .

. . . and jumps on the chair. Freddy's box is on the table.

Lily jumps. *Splash!* She falls in the pan of water.

"We have to get away," says Lily. "The Man wants to eat you."
"Oh, Lily," says Freddy. "I don't want to be a prince anymore.
Let's go back to the pond."

Lily and Freddy try to jump out of the box, but the sides are too high.

"Now we are both stuck in my castle," says Freddy.

"You should never give up hope," Lily says.

"What's going on in here?" says the boy, who has come back into the room. "I'm glad to hear you're getting better, little frog." But when he looks in the box . . .

. . .and sees the two of them he is so surprised he drops the box on the floor. Two frogs jump out and run around the room . . .

. . . and two pairs of green legs
disappear out the window.

"I hope you learned something, Freddy," says Lily.
"I did," says Freddy. "I learned you're brave, Lily."